First published in 2013
by Hodder Children's Books.

Copyright © Mick Inkpen 2013

Hodder Children's Books
338 Euston Road, London NW1 3BH

Hodder Children's Books Australia
Level 17/207 Kent Street, Sydney, NSW 2000

The right of Mick Inkpen to be identified as the author
and illustrator of this Work has been asserted by him in
accordance with the Copyright, Designs and Patents Act 1988.

A catalogue record of this book is
available from the British Library.

ISBN: 978 1 444 91223 4
10 9 8 7 6 5 4 3 2 1

Printed in China

Hodder Children's Books is a
division of Hachette Children's Books,
an Hachette UK Company
www.hachette.co.uk

Wibbly Pig

and the Tooky

Mick Inkpen

Hodder
Children's
Books

A division of Hachette Children's Books

'Hello
Wibbly!
Look what I've got!'

Big Pig's sister and
her friend have been
to the zoo.
Big Pig's sister's
friend has bought a
cuddly koala at the
gift shop.

'I think I'll call him
KOOKy,' she says.

'That's **nothing!**'
says Big Pig's sister.
'Look what
I've got!
His name is
Tooky.'

'Wow, he looks
almost real!' says
Wibbly Pig.

Wrark!

rk! Wrark! Wrark!

'How do you
make him do that?'
says Wibbly Pig.
'And where do the
batteries go?
And how much does
a Tooky cost?'

The Tooky pecks
Wibbly Pig's finger.
Ouch!

Tooky is not a toy.
Tooky is a toucan.
A real toucan.

'He's real, silly!'
says Big Pig's sister.
'And he likes bananas.
Have you got any?'

'We're not
supposed
to bring the
animals home,'
says Big Pig's
sister's friend.

'He wanted me to,'
says Big Pig's sister.
'And he loves me,
don't you,
Tooky Wooky?'

The toucan pecks
her on the nose.

'My dose!
My dose!'
she shrieks.

She makes
such a fuss
she frightens
the toucan. . .   which goes flapping

'ound the room!'

'I don't want
him any more.
You have him!'
she squeals.

It takes ages to
catch the toucan.
But he calms down
when Big Pig's sister's
friend gives him her
cuddly koala
to play with.

'Tooky
and Kooky!'
she says.

'He'll have to
go back,' says
Wibbly Pig.

So they dress him up and put a hat over his head to keep him quiet on the bus. 'Nobody will guess he's real now,' says Wibbly Pig.

But how do they keep his beak shut?

With one of
Big Pig's sister's ribbons.

She isn't very
happy about that.

'What I don't understand,' says Wibbly Pig, 'is how we get him back in the bird house.'

'We don't,' says Big Pig's sister. 'We just wait till Toucan Teatime. They bring them all out for their dinner. Easy peasy.'

At the zoo the sign says,
'Toucan Teatime 3PM.'
'It's past 3 already!'
says Wibbly Pig. 'They'll soon
be finished! Hurry!'

But Big Pig's
sister isn't listening.
She has spotted
something much
more interesting.

'See you later!'
she says.

Toucan Teatime **3pm** →

← **3:15** Penguin Party

Llama Llunch **3:30** ↗

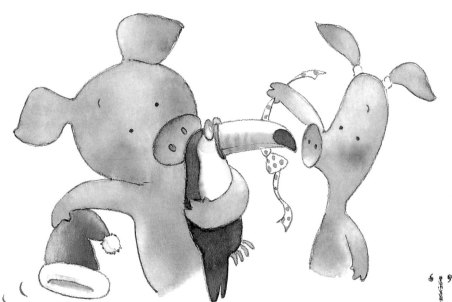

The toucans have nearly finished their tea.

'I'll hold Tooky. You grab the ribbon,' says Wibbly Pig. 'Don't let him peck you!'

Wibbly Pig whips off the hat and plonks Tooky back on his perch.

'I think we forgot
something,' giggles
Big Pig's sister's friend.

Big Pig's sister arrives. She is looking very pleased with herself.

She grabs her ribbon and puts it back on.

'Toucans are so **yesterday**,' she says.

'Where have you been?' says Wibbly Pig. 'And what's that **fishy** smell?'

'And where is
your other ribbon?'
says Big Pig's
sister's friend.

'Time to go!'
says Big Pig's sister.